Blood Song

ALSO BY ERIC DROOKER

Flood!: A Novel in Pictures

Illuminated Poems (with Allen Ginsberg)

Street Posters & Ballads

Blood Song

A SILENT BALLAD

ERIC DROOKER

Introduction by Joe Sacco

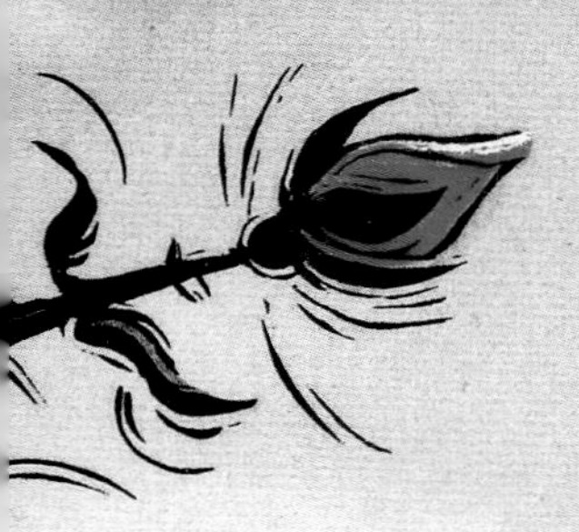

A Harvest Original
HARCOURT, INC.
San Diego New York London

Requests for permission to make copies of any part of the work should be mailed to the following address: Permissions Department, Harcourt, Inc., 6277 Sea Harbor Drive, Orlando, Florida 32887-6777.

www.HarcourtBooks.com

Library of Congress Cataloging-in-Publication Data
Drooker, Eric, 1958–
Blood song: a silent ballad/Eric Drooker; introduction by Joe Sacco.
p. cm.
"A harvest original."
ISBN 0-15-600884-X
1. Drooker, Eric, 1958– 2. Stories without words. I. Title.
NC139.D76 A4 2002
760'.092—dc21 2002024263

The author wishes to thank the following people: André Bernard, Jen Charat, Emma Coleman, Paula Hewitt, Jenessa Paige and Siddhartha, Mumia Abu-Jamal, Alli Starr, Mike Tofu, Sarah Ludwig, Trish Overstreet, Chris Zimmerman, Vera, Ernest, Joel, and Alejandro Ernesto Ludwig Doerfler, and Nina, Harold, Star, Jessie, and Rain Drooker...and the millions...

Text set in Neue Neuland
Display type hand-lettered by Eric Drooker
Cover and interior art by Eric Drooker
Artwork engraved in scratchboard and watercolored
Designed by Eric Drooker and Linda Lockowitz

Printed in Singapore
First Harvest edition 2002

A C E G I J K H F D B

For Emma . . .

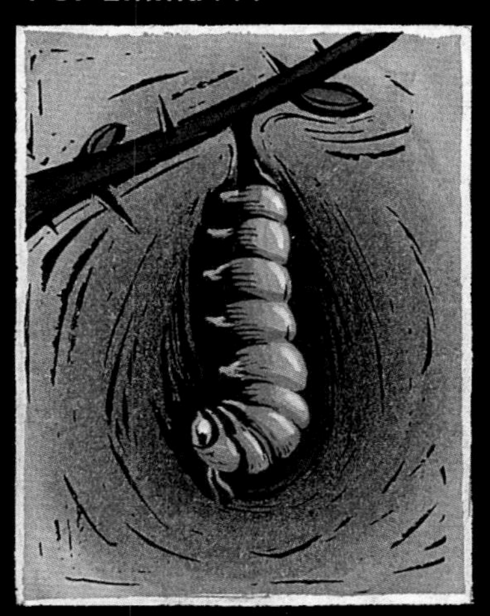

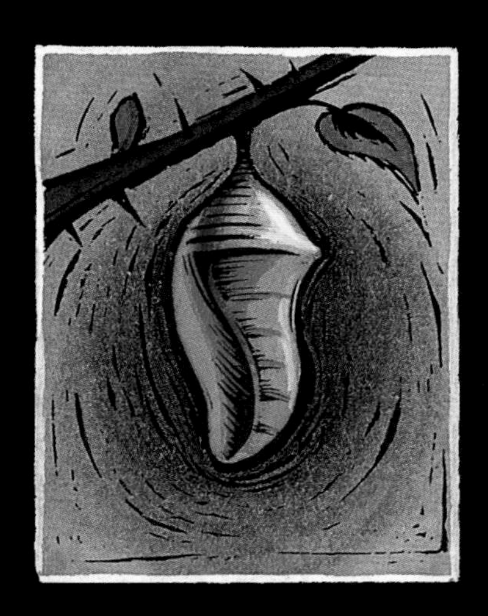

Introduction

I MET ERIC DROOKER only once for a few short hours six or seven years ago in New York City. Over drinks, Drooker, this far-out, far-left, street-wise artist, held me spellbound with stories of the outbursts and upheavals that have punctuated the Lower East Side's dense political history, which, clearly, was his own. Walking me back to the subway station, Drooker motioned to doorways and street corners, describing what had happened there five or fifteen or 100 years ago as if those things were happening before his eyes again and now. No person I have met since has seemed as organically from a place, not simply by virtue of his being born, raised, and schooled there, but because his streets also teemed with long dead and mostly forgotten characters who had lived and ached and struggled, too, and from whose lives he was still able to draw much meaning.

At the time, Drooker was known to me as one of the New York cabal of activist cartoonists and poster artists, which included Peter Kuper and Seth Tobocman, who had joined forces on the oversized anthology of political comics, *World War 3 Illustrated.* And I knew Drooker's wordless narrative, *Flood!: A Novel in Pictures,* then recently released and the recipient of an American Book Award. *Flood!*'s powerful images of confrontation between protesters and police were informed by Drooker's own physical batterings in the city's campaign-by-truncheon to sort out the punks and squatters and whores and homeless people who were among his neighbors and, incidentally, not in step with some grander, happy-faced vision of a well-scrubbed populace for a well-scrubbed New York.

In some ways, *Blood Song* is a companion to *Flood!,* a refining of those same themes, but this is a story of greater scope, its starting point, in fact, images of the universe and then the earth and then a pastoral, mountainous landscape far removed from the skyscraper heights and valleys that dominate Drooker's previous settings.

Where are we here? Southeast Asia? And when? An idyllic time, perhaps, when villagers took only what they needed and left their surroundings as they found them.

But we are in for surprises and jolts as Drooker pushes his story squarely into a modern, more ruthless age and from one landscape to another, each strikingly familiar but none wholly identifiable. Drooker's images seem to invoke settings that are more general than specific, emphasizing that this is not the story of one or two places, but of the opposing life-affirming and life-crushing forces that rage wherever people live on our planet.

Set against *Blood Song*'s themes of regeneration, rebirth, and resistance is the brute power of armies and police forces that do the bidding of vested interests. Drooker's real accomplishment is that he tells this modern story without words, using an ancient form of communication, one that relies on pictures to record stories (think Egyptian tomb paintings or the picture manuscripts of pre-Columbian Central America, for example). Without the interpretive filter of words, relying solely on the images and their sequence, we comprehend Drooker's narrative immediately and viscerally. He is granting us a direct line into the heart of the female protagonist.

In the words of Belgian expressionist Frans Masereel, who produced several woodcut novels over fifty years and is Drooker's obvious modern antecedent, "art is in the first place communication addressed to all men." But in reaching "all men" artistry is needed, and much is owed to the masterly way Drooker has constructed his tale, his exquisite sense of pacing, and the clarity of his images.

Each scratchboard-etched and watercolored image in *Blood Song* works in sequential step to drive the story forward, and yet each could stand alone as a work of art. The drawings of mountains, seas, and urban streets are breathtaking. Drooker's use of light and dark accentuate mood, and his occasional and precise touches of color in this black-and-blue tale are refreshing to the point of invoking joy. For all the glories of Drooker's previous work, *Flood!*, that book was partly a proving ground, a place where he learned his craft. *Blood Song* is the work of an artist of the first order at his maturity.

The aforementioned Masereel, whose work Drooker first discovered at age twelve (courtesy of his grandfather, an old-school socialist), was a pacifist who fled to Switzerland rather than participate in the carnage of the First World War. He would have approved not only Drooker's revival of the wordless medium, but his engagement in the real world against the backdrop of snickering complacency. Said Masereel, "I cannot conceive of an artist isolating himself in an ivory tower, this seems anti-human, and, in any case out of keeping with our way of life. . . . The artist is in the very front rank of those who lead humanity toward a better world, more beautiful, more free, more just, more brotherly."

It is just this sort of idyllic hope, amidst the enormous ugliness and brutality of our worse nature that lies at *Blood Song*'s heart. Years ago, when I met Drooker, he seemed so much from New York's Lower East Side. That much is probably still true. But with this work about oppression and the struggle against it on two sides of an ocean, Drooker seems to come from the rest of the world, too.

—Joe Sacco

New York City

March 2002

"Dust to dust, and blood for blood—
Passion and pangs! Has Time
Gone back? or is this the Age
Of the world's great Prime?"

—Herman Melville

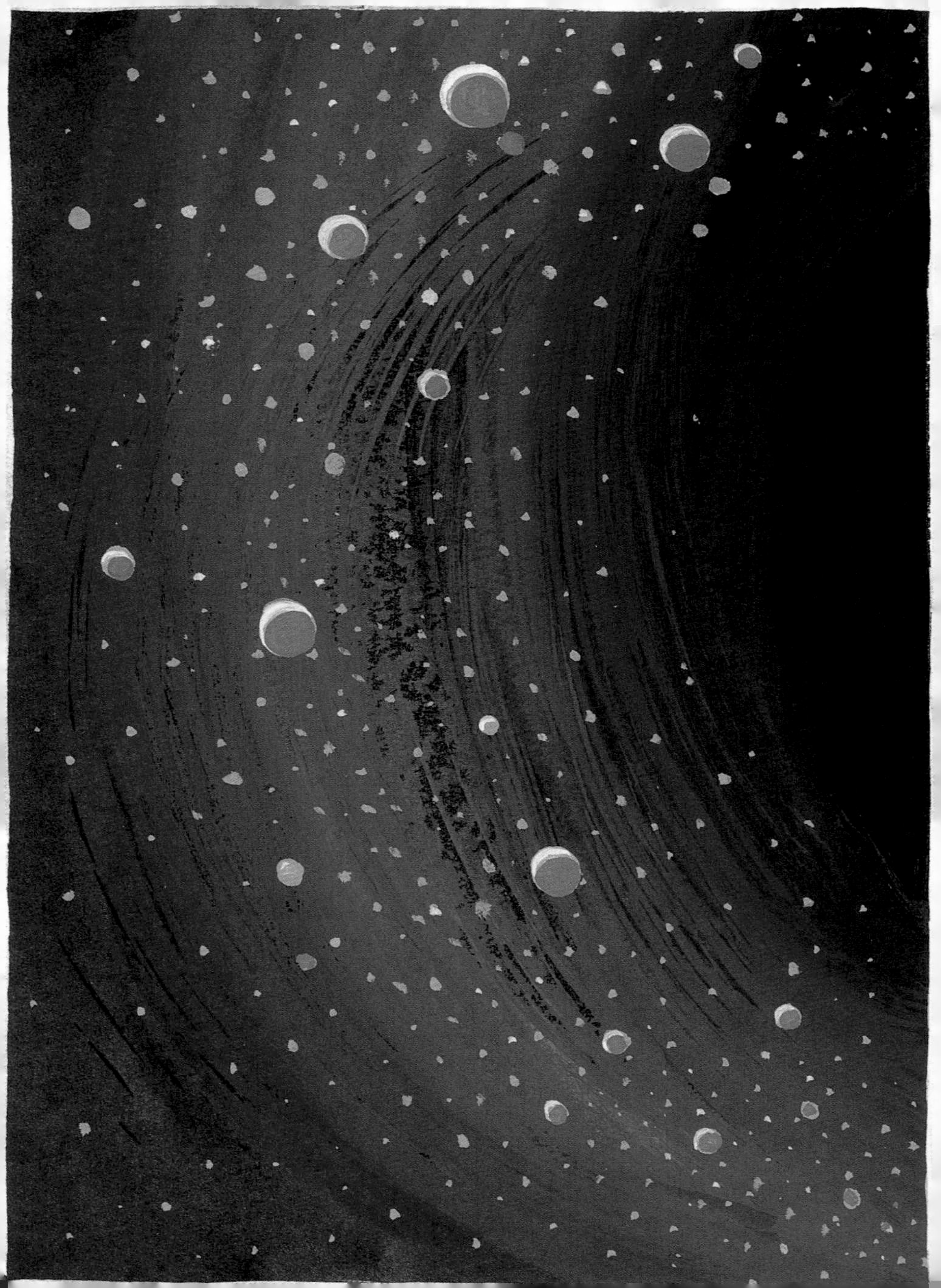

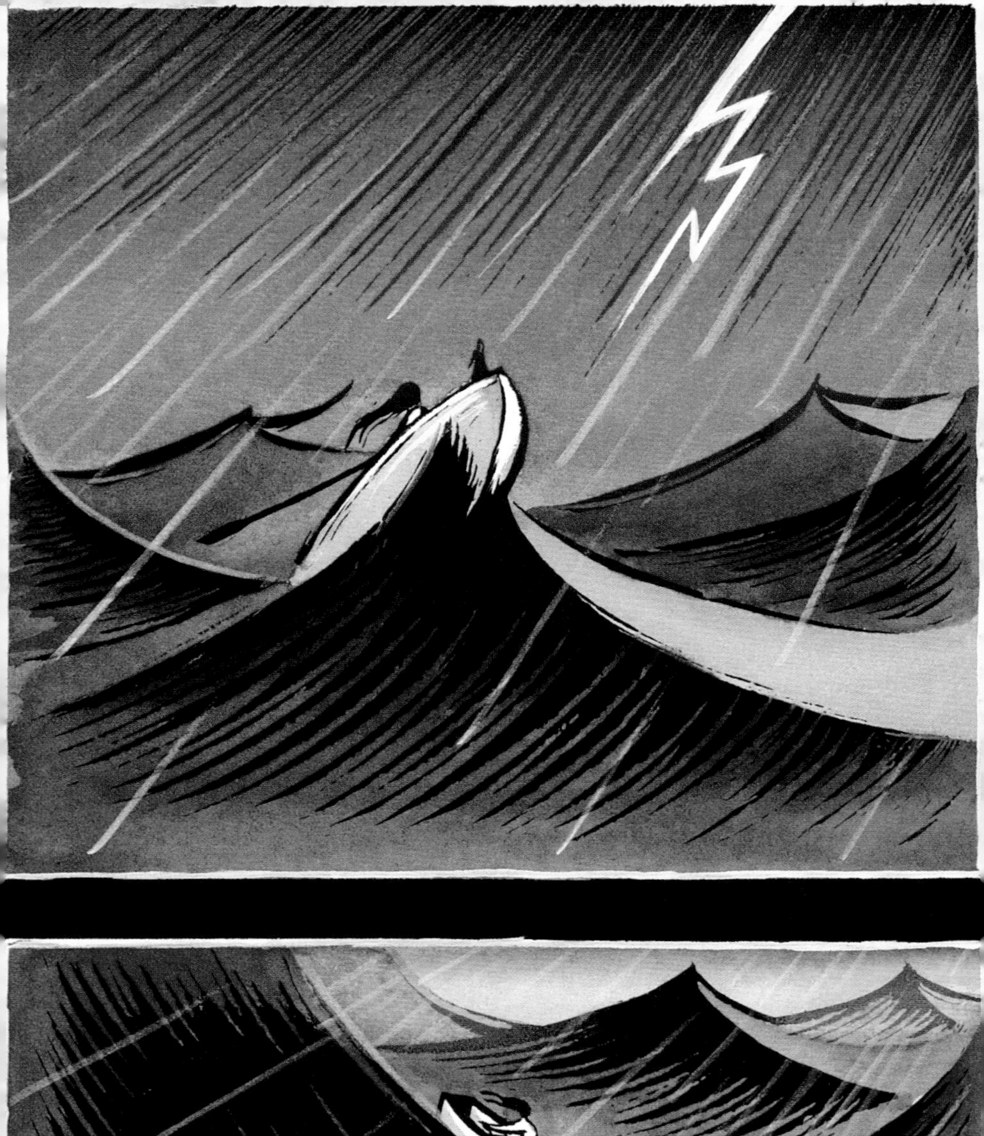

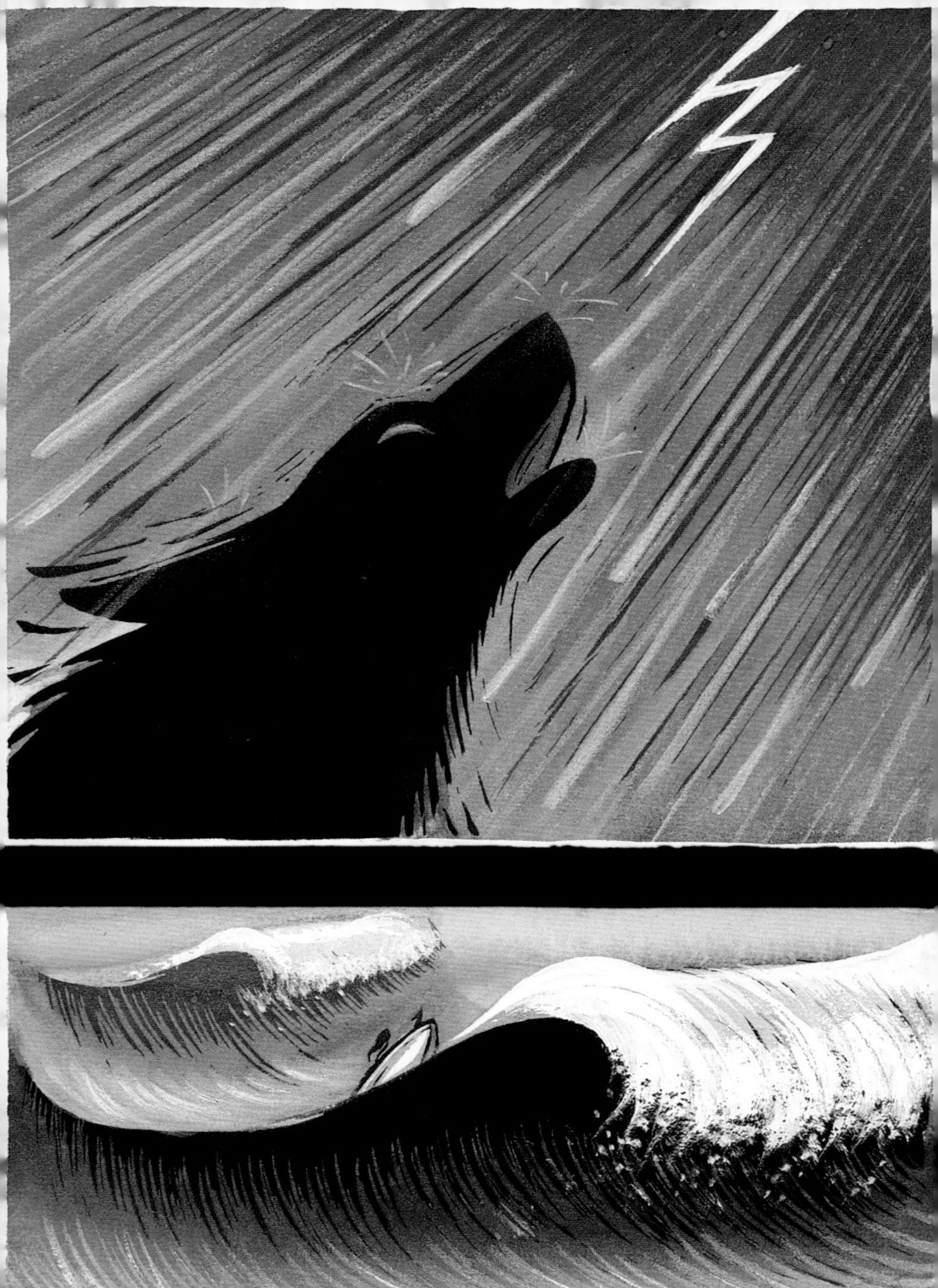

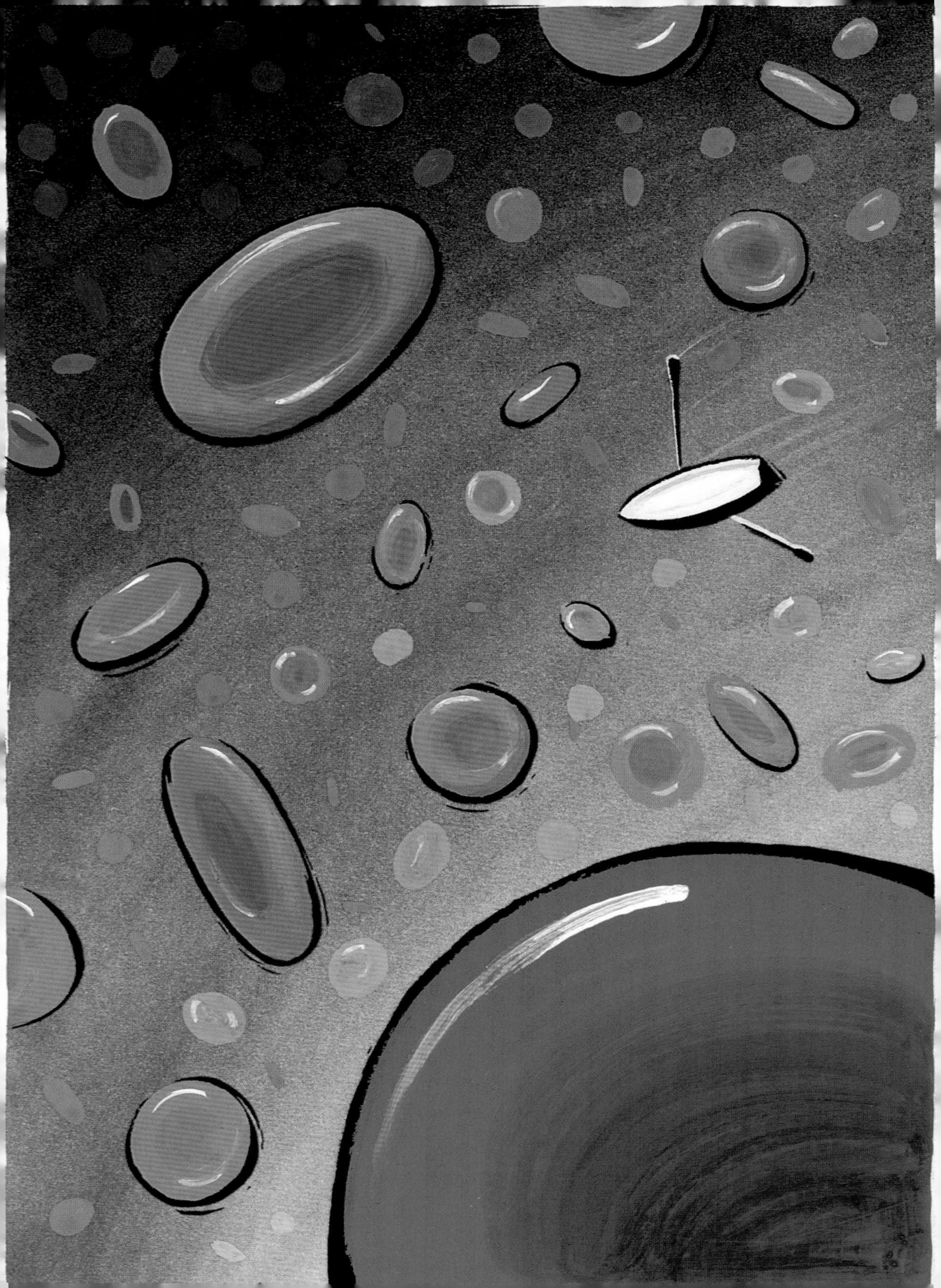

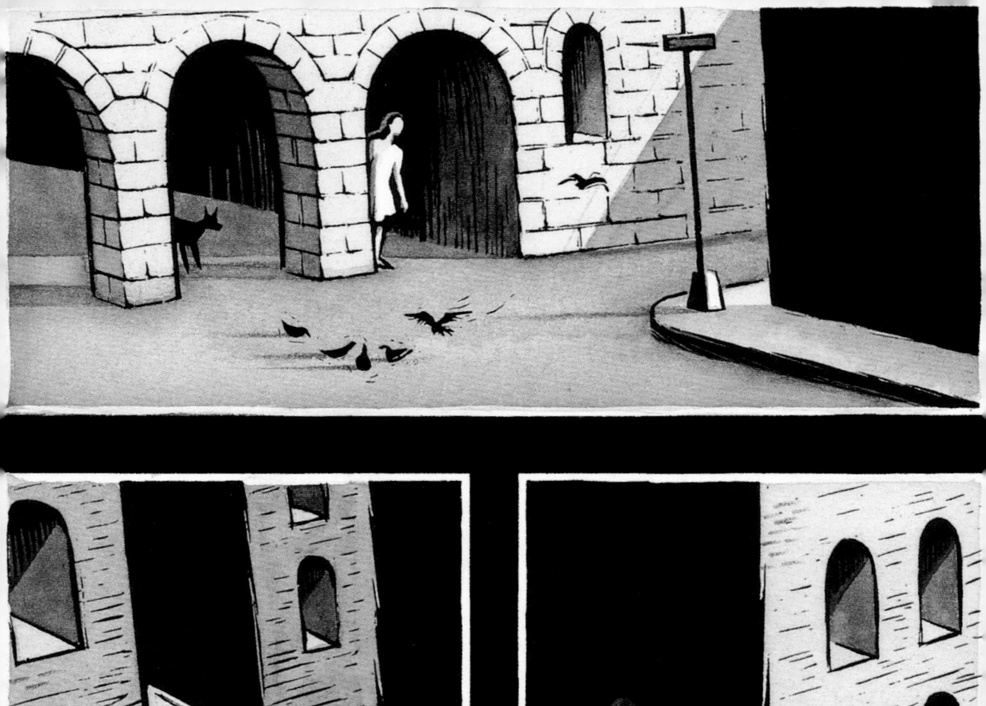

BROADWAY
KING

KING